STEPHANIE MARIE
DARK ROMANCE AUTHOR

Logan,
If we catch you,
we fuck you!

heathens
HOLLOW

Copyright

ALL RIGHTS RESERVED.

No part of this publication may be reproduced, distributed, or transmitted in any form or by any means, including photocopying, recording, or other electronic or mechanical methods, without the prior written permission of the publisher.

This is a work of fiction. Any resemblance of characters to actual persons, living or dead, is purely coincidental. Stephanie Marie holds exclusive rights to this work.

Unauthorized duplication is prohibited.

Copyright © 2024 by Stephanie Marie

Dear Reader

HEATHENS HOLLOW is a short novella.

*This is a dark and spicy background story from the characters in **THE KINGS OF DESTRUCTION** series.*

Please note this is a Dark Romance.

Some subjects and scenes may be triggering for some. Please ensure that you read the Trigger Warnings on the next page.

Want more spice and dark romances?

Come join us in Stephanie Marie's Book Babes

Come and say hi. We can't wait to see you there!!

Triggers

I would like to say thank you first of all for picking up a copy of **HEATHENS HOLLOW**.

Please remember that this is a short Novella with a Halloween theme, giving you a little backstory on the characters in my upcoming **KINGS OF DESTRUCTION SERIES**.

NO HEA happens in this book!

As this is a **DARK ROMANCE** you may find some themes/subjects triggering.

These are but not subject to:

~ ON PAGE/ TOPIC OF DEATH
~ STALKER
~ MENTAL/VERBAL ABUSE
~KNIFE PLAY
~CAPTIVITY
~ NON-CON / DUB CON

Dedication

Tell me someone who doesn't want masked men to chase them through the woods at Halloween, wreaking havoc on your body while calling you a good girl.

Praise me, daddy!

1

Emilie

The crisp autumn leaves fall against my window as I bring my truck to a slow and steady stop before killing the engine. My hands tremble and slip, loosening on the wheel as they grow cold and clammy.

I throw my head back and close my eyes while trying to visualize an alternate universe, but nothing materializes. Nothing but a mixture of raw emotions thrumming deep in my veins, wreaking havoc on my body. Emotions I've been working so hard to keep pushed down, refusing to acknowledge them ever since my world turned to shit. I don't know why I bother because no matter how hard I try to fight it; the end result always remains the same.

As much as I'd love to, I can't dream this one away. Believe me, I've tried a thousand times. Instead, my heart continues to pound its vicious assault on my chest...*boom... boom... boom...*

Relentless and unapologetic. A mirror image of the unforgiving world around me. Each wicked beat a painful reminder of what's been lost... of what's been taken from me. A silent reminder to compose myself before I'm forced to toughen up and face the music.

I shouldn't be here.

This shouldn't be happening, period. Sure, I can try to pretend all I damn well want that this isn't happening. That this is nothing more than one of my bad dreams, but I also know that when I open my eyes again, the small, quaint churchyard will be waiting for me. Proving that this hideous nightmare is now my reality. A reality I need to get used to and fast.

Biting down on my lower lip, forcing myself to focus on anything but my unshed tears as they threaten to spill over, I cast my eyes toward the barren trees which surround me, watching as they sway, fighting an impossible battle with the vicious winds as the storm clouds roll in above me—the sky darkening with each passing second, much like what's left of my soul. A sure sign that summer is behind us and the cold, dark nights are beginning to close in.

Fall used to be my favorite time of year but now it's so much more than the monsters hiding out in the shadows which haunt me.

It's crazy how fast things can change. In the blink of an eye everything I'd ever known has changed, removed, and forever lost, and now I'm the one who's been left behind as I try to navigate my way through the endless flood of my grief; desperately trying to cling on; to survive this turmoil.

I feel betrayed knowing that the sun will still set and give way to the night. The seasons will continue to change. Just another heartless reminder that no matter what's happened inside my little bubble, life doesn't stop for anyone. It continues to move on.

The universe doesn't care that my world has ended. She doesn't give a fuck about me and my issues, and that majorly pisses me off.

A tap sounds on my truck window, pulling me out of my thoughts and a wave of relief washes over me when I find my best friend waiting for me.

Fuck... I'm not ready for this. I don't think I'll ever be ready, but I also know that I can't put it off any longer. Just like the world won't stop for me, I can't deny the inevitable. Breathing in deep I pull my leather jacket tight around my body in a last-ditch attempt to keep myself together—just for a little while.

Nausea consumes me as I open the door, the cold having zero effect on my numb body as I climb out of my truck before kicking the door shut with the back of my black boots.

"I drove by the house on the way here," Skylar tells me and there's no judgment in her voice but I don't miss the pity flashing in her deep chocolate brown eyes. "But you weren't there."

Anxiously I chew my lips, trying to divert my attention to anything other than the reason why we're here on a cold October morning.

"Why didn't you wait for me?" Her tone is calm and full of nothing but genuine concern. I know she's worried about me. Fuck, even I'm worried about me, but it will have to wait because today isn't about me. I have all the time in the world to deal with my issues so holding out another day isn't going to damage me anymore than I already am.

Shaking my head, I pull my arms tight around my waist, trying and failing to contain the pain to one place. Desperate to ease the dull ache building deep within my chest. "I'm sorry. I know we'd already agreed, but I couldn't stay there. I had to get out of that house." The words fall freely. "I needed to be alone with my thoughts for a little while."

Skylar reaches out, her arms wrapping around me, holding me close, always letting me know that she has my back no matter what life decides to throw my way.

"Did it help?"

I shake my head, unable to speak as my throat constricts against the emotions battling within me.

"I get it." She soothes, rubbing my back. Calming me in the way that only she can. "Whatever you need, you know I've always got you." Squeezing me tight, she keeps my fragile body together and I close my eyes, needing the comfort more than she'll ever know. I inhale, breathing her in. I savor her floral scent, committing it to memory and my heart shatters some more because deep down I already know that this right here; this is most likely to be my last true feeling of home for a while. I selfishly savor every stolen second so I can come back to this feeling whenever I want. Whenever I need a little comfort and reassurance.

A firm reminder of who I am and what I had.

"How the fuck did we even get here?" I whisper, my eyes darting to the gray and gloomy sky, searching for answers. Answers that I'll never get. At least not in this lifetime. Of course, I knew this day would come eventually. I guess I just didn't think it would happen so soon. I foolishly thought we'd have more time. Just a little longer, but she was taken away from me too soon. Before either of us were ready to say goodbye.

The scuffle of feet sounds out, alerting me to a presence behind me and Skylar pulls away before clearing her throat.

"Miss Garcia, I'm so sorry for your loss." Turing ever so slowly I come face to face with Father O'Hare, and my heart drops to the pit of my stomach as the finality hits me hard in the chest, knocking all the air from my lungs, leaving me breathless.

I don't have the words to respond so I offer him a small nod instead, hoping he doesn't find me rude and ignorant.

"We're ready to begin."

Once again, I find myself fighting against my tears as they threaten to spill over for the hundredth time today as he bows his head, his white hair shining bright like a halo on his head. Even in this moment, the irony isn't lost on me.

Clearing my throat, I use everything I have to find my voice again. "Thank you, Father" I nod, signaling for him to proceed. I force one weak leg in front of the other and before I have a chance to stumble or fall, Skylar links her arm in mine, holding me steady as I walk into the hardest moment of my life.

2

Emilie

The small church is empty aside from me, Skylar, Father O'Hare and the wooden casket up front, perfectly positioned before the altar. A warm, rich aroma fills the air as the priest wafts incense around my mother's coffin as me and Skylar make our way down the aisle.

'In the arms of the angel' plays out around us, another reminder that this isn't one of my nightmares. This is real. This is happening.

"Where is everyone?" Skylar whispers as we take our rightful seats on the front bench.

"I warned them all to stay away." I reply flatly, zero emotion seeping into my voice.

Skylar's eyes narrow as she looks at me in confusion. "But didn't she…"

"They weren't here for her when she was alive…" I cut her off and I don't even feel bad about it. "So why should they get to be here for her in death?"

I'm angry. I'm beyond upset and even though I'm riddled with grief right now I mean every fucking word. No one in our family was around for us when we needed them. None of our so-called family and friends gave a shit about us. I think that was clear for everyone to see. They knew what was going down. They all knew because I told them in the hope that they might actually step up and look after one of their own, maybe even show up in my mom's hour of need.

Did they show? Did they fuck. From that moment I decided to handle everything myself. They showed us just how much we mattered to them with their absence. Actions sure speak louder than words and I'm not the type of person to play nice just to keep up appearances. They won't get to dine out on my mom's illness, or her expense. Especially when she's no longer here to defend herself.

My life has always consisted of me, my mom and Skylar for as long as I can remember and we did just fine. It feels right that it's just us here for my mom's final goodbye. Anything other than this would have felt fake and orchestrated.

"In the name of the father..." The music stops as the priest opens up the mass and my eyes instantly zone in on my mom's wooden casket. My chest tightens, crushing me and stealing what little air I have left. *"...and of the son, and of the holy spirit..."*

"Breathe." Skylar whispers, placing her hand in mine, holding me close.

I'm trying. Really, I am. But fuck me, this is a whole lot harder than I thought it would be. My mind is fully aware of what's happening, but it's like it's trying to block out the severity of the situation. Like it's trying to shield and protect me from any further damage.

"We're gathered here today to celebrate the short yet beautiful life of Hannah Garcia..."

I zone out. I hear the priest speaking in the distance but it's distorted. Like my head has been plunged underwater, and a part of me is thankful for the small reprieve.

A year. One year minimum they said. Specialists my ass. They promised us. They looked us straight in the eye and assured us we'd have one last Christmas together. A chance for us to make more memories. Ones that I'd be able to cherish forever. Bullshit. What they told us was nothing but dead promises and empty lies. Each and every one of them were full of shit, no doubt telling the patient and her distraught child what they wanted to hear so they could get rid of them faster.

After that last conversation with my mom's consultant, she was dead within two weeks. No added illnesses. No sudden spike in temperature or infection. We didn't have a single warning sign to tell me she was slipping away faster than we could have ever imagined.

I woke up last Thursday morning to find that she'd gone. Peacefully in her sleep, unknowingly leaving me afraid and all alone in this big wide world. A world I now have to navigate on my own.

3

Emilie

The service passed me by in a blur of hidden memories.

I don't even remember coming outside and laying my mom to rest. It must have happened because I vaguely remember Skylar holding me close before I told her to go on without me.

The truth is, I'm not ready to leave my mom just yet. I'm not ready to say my final goodbye and the thought of my mom being out here, all alone, six feet deep in the ground has me feeling unsettled. On edge.

Thankfully Skylar didn't ask any questions. She gave me a reassuring hug and told me that she'd be happy to wait until I was ready to go, no matter how long that might be. I didn't want her waiting around. I already felt like a burden as it is. I wanted to be alone. I needed to be alone. She finally left after I'd promised to call her when I was on my way back to the house.

Our cemetery is situated in the little church of *St Mary's* in our small town and I'm not surprised to find it empty. Father O'Hare must have locked up for the day and nothing but the sound of the leaves rustling in the wind keeps me company.

"I'm so sorry, mom." I say on a breathless whisper as I lower my body to the ground, imagining that I'm sitting on the side of her bed the way I used to do. I feel the first hot, salty tear roll down my cheek and I don't try to fight it this time. I'm done fighting. I close my eyes as I allow them to fall freely. It feels strange. I've held everything in for so long. I've buried every emotion possible and now they're erupting. I have no way of containing it.

I don't want to cry. I don't want to show any form of weakness. I need to prove to my mom that no matter how hard things get, I've got this. I want to prove that through my pain and indescribable heartache I can still hold my own. But it's all proving too much to handle.

"Emilie." A familiar voice calls out from behind me and my stomach knots. What the fuck does he think he's playing at? My mom's just been lowered into the ground and he suddenly thinks this is the perfect opportunity for small talk? Nothing should surprise me anymore, but why can't he see that I just want to be left alone, caught up in my thoughts as I sit with my mom.

"I don't want to talk to you." I grit out through clenched teeth, refusing to turn around. Refusing to acknowledge his unwelcome presence.

"Emilie, please. We need to talk."

"Like fuck we do." I hurl back as a fresh wave of pain rolls through me, crippling deep in my stomach.

"Look, I know you're upset..." he begins while stepping closer and placing his hand on my shoulder, and just like that my trance has been broken. Without another thought I push myself up from the ground and turn to face him, my heart hammering deep inside my chest and it all becomes too much. Something inside me snaps.

"Upset?" I hurl, refusing to curb my anger as I lunge for him, my fists banging against his chest as he tries and fails to restrain me. "You don't know the first fucking thing about being upset so don't you dare stand there and patronize me."

"Emilie, please." He presses but it's too late. I don't want to look at him, let alone listen to his bullshit. I've experienced years of that already, which only tells me one thing: he's going to start talking whether I want him to or not. "Calm down and listen to me."

Daniel: my so-called boyfriend, has always been the master manipulator. He has this magical ability to twist and turn any situation on its head, perfectly making it all about him and how he's feeling. So why should today be any different?

The truth is, right now I couldn't give two fucks about how Daniel is feeling. His emotions, or lack of them are completely irrelevant to me. Null and fucking void, and I can't see that changing anytime soon—if ever.

Another fresh wave of anger surges, bubbling deep in my chest as I take a step back and take him in. I feel sick. This is the guy who at one time meant everything to me. Only it turns out I didn't mean shit to him. I was blinded for a while, but now I see him perfectly… in all his nasty glory.

Daniel has fooled people from the get-go. He's picture perfect. Tall. Tan. Fair-haired, with the most captivating blue eyes. The perfect mask for a monster. Beneath his beauty is an emotionless beast who preys on everyone around him. Stealing all their energy to fuel him. To give his ego the boost it needs. The boost he craves. If life isn't all about Daniel then he doesn't want any part of it.

For years I stupidly believed that Daniel was the one. I believed he was my person. My be all and end all. *My future.* My life. But fuck me, how wrong was I. Over time his true colors started to show. The odd comment here, a little degrading there. Sadly, by that point I'd found I was making excuses for him. Trying to justify his words and actions. Convincing myself that he didn't mean any of it. We were just going through a tough patch, like most couples and I thought it would pass and we'd be fine.

It's funny how it takes something drastic to happen to snap your eyes wide open.

"Why are you here?" I demand, folding my arms over my chest, refusing to let him in.

His blue eyes narrow as his own hands slide deep into his jean pockets before rocking back and forth on the heels of his trainers. I shouldn't be surprised but it stings a little knowing he didn't even bother to dress for the occasion. If my mom could see him now, she'd be disgusted.

Sure, he didn't bother to attend her funeral, and that's because he's a heartless bastard. Plus, my mom dying before her time isn't anything to do with him, but I'm sure he's busy thinking about ways he can try to turn this all around on him. Maybe he thinks he's in the right but all I can see is him standing at her graveside, the soil not even settled while being his usual disrespectful self.

"I came to see you." He sounds so sincere that anyone could be fooled into believing he actually means the constant stream of bullshit which falls from his mouth. But not me. Not anymore. "All I want to do is talk and make sure that you're okay."

"I think you said everything you needed last week when you told me to hurry up and drop dead like my mom." I remind him, my voice steady, holding a lot more conviction than I feel, and I'm caught off guard when he flinches at my words.

"Emilie, baby..." He takes one step forward, causing me to take one back and I'm getting closer to stepping on my mom's grave. "You know I didn't mean a word of what was said. I was upset... grieving... and you kept pulling away from me."

"You were grieving. Correct me if I'm wrong but did you lose your mom too?" I knew it would only be a matter of time before he started to twist it and make this about him. I'm stronger than I used to be and I know how his mind games work. I refuse to fall victim to him again.

"I cared about her too." I see his crocodile tears glistening in his eyes as he tries to up the ante. I wish he could see himself through my eyes and he'd see just how sad and pathetic he really is.

"Ha…" I throw my head back and laugh. This guy is something else and the more I look at him the more I wonder what I fucking saw in him in the first place. "You, caring about someone? The only person you care about is yourself."

"I didn't mean it…"

"Yeah, just like you didn't mean to fall into Natalie's bed and end up fucking her when things got tough, either."

His brows furrow, pissed that I'd have the audacity to bring up his cheating ways again. I'd like to say I've forgiven and forgotten but neither would be true. Daniel was the one who did the dirty so he best believe I'll bring it up whenever the fuck I want, because I can. He is not the injured party here.

"We've been through this already. I thought we'd moved on?"

Another laugh escapes me. He just keeps leveling up with his bullshit and I have no idea where it's going to end. "Moved on? Are you being serious right now?" Shaking my head, utter disbelief floods through my body. I don't even have the words right now. "Have you heard yourself? You're still talking about something that's completely irrelevant. Something which has nothing to do with the here and now. Have you ever stopped to think what I've just been through, or am I suddenly supposed to dust myself off and act like everything is fine because she's been lowered into the ground?"

Daniel watches me for a moment, contemplating his next move before he offers me a small nod, pretending to act like he understands what I've had to go through and it does nothing to ease my mood, instead it makes my anger bubble some more.

"Fuck you, Daniel. You don't have any idea. You can pretend all you like but the truth is you don't know how it feels. You have no idea what I'm going through, and why should you when the only thing you've ever lost is your self-respect and any dignity you had left. But then I guess that's what happens when you start putting shit up your nose. You become the drug and the drug becomes you, destroying everything around you in the process."

The pain of his endless betrayals still hurt. As much as I would love to forget him and pretend he didn't exist, my mind and heart won't allow me that luxury. He's imprinted deep in my mind, a lesson never to lose myself to another man ever again. I am enough, and I deserve so much better than him.

The longer I stand here, trapped in this deadly stalemate with the boy who broke my heart, the more I'm wishing I didn't send Skylar away. I didn't think it would be a problem. I never expected Daniel to turn up. I made it perfectly clear that I didn't want him here and a part of me honestly thought he'd be too busy trying to score or drowning his sorrows to even remember what was happening.

My shoulders sag as a heavy, weary sigh escapes me and I know he doesn't miss it. "Why don't you do us both a favor and just go home Daniel." I move to walk away but he's faster than I anticipated as he reaches out before gripping my arm, digging his fingers in and pulling me close.

"I came here to talk to you," he growls, his nasty side starting to surface. "Don't you dare try to walk away and disrespect me." Attacking me in a graveyard next to my mother's grave clearly isn't beneath him. Maybe I was right about him trying to score because the Daniel I knew, even though vicious and manipulative, he would never act out like this in public. Not sober anyway.

"Get off me." I bite, making him dig his fingers deeper into my flesh. His face twists in disgust, his nostrils flaring. Daniel has always despised anyone standing up to him and I'm no exception.

"This isn't over, Emilie. You don't get to walk away from me." His voice is laced with venom as his mask slips some more, exposing the true monster within.

"Oh, trust me... it is so over, and the sooner you accept that the better it will be, for the both of us."

His free hand grips the back of my neck as he pulls me closer to him, cementing his hold on me, silently warning me that things are about to switch, but I no longer care what he does or doesn't do to me. My mom dying changed me in so many ways. I'm numb. Void of any emotion. I'm like an empty shell of my former self, and I don't even recognize who I am anymore. My heart no longer beats as it once did, full of life and endless possibilities. The change in me isn't because Daniel betrayed me in every way imaginable. He holds zero control over me now. No, the change is because the one person who loved me the most in all the world, unconditionally and unapologetically, has gone. She's been taken away from me in the cruelest way and no matter how hard I pray; she's never coming back. Not in this lifetime, anyway.

"You don't get to end this, Emilie. You belong to me and me alone."

"I'm not your possession. I don't belong to anyone."

"What more do you want from me? What else do I have to do to prove to you that I care. I'm here, aren't I? I thought that's what you wanted?"

"I did. That's all I ever wanted," I confess as he loosens his grip on my hair. "But not anymore." Surprisingly the truth falls from my lips with ease and I don't even feel bad about it. I used to hate it when he got all confrontational, staying quiet to help defuse a bad situation, but those days are long behind me. "It's too late, Daniel."

"You… you don't mean that." He exclaims, his eyes growing wide as another rush of anger sweeps through his body. I watch as he juts his chin, the sharp tick of his jaw as he struggles to keep a handle on his emotions. "You belong with me, and you know it." Tilting his head to the side, he looks over at my mom's final resting place. "This is what she would have wanted. Me and you together, supporting each other through our loss."

"Don't you fucking dare." I warn as adrenaline courses through my veins, my fight or flight kicking in. "How fucked up are you? My mom is my loss, not yours and as far as I can remember you haven't supported me through shit. My mom didn't even like you."

"You're lying..."

"I'm not. My mom finally saw through you. She saw you for the nasty, controlling piece of shit you've always been. I was just to blind and naive to see it."

He drops his other hand and takes a step back, pain etched onto his angular face, but I'm not buying it. I'm happy I've finally got some kind of reaction out of him, but we both know it's not genuine. Daniel doesn't give a shit about anyone's opinions. "She wouldn't say that."

"Oh, she did... and so much more, but I don't think it's fair to voice it, especially when she's no longer here to back it up."

He shakes his head, refusing to listen to what I've just said. "It would have been the medication. She would have confused me with some other deadbeat from your family."

"You'd love that, wouldn't you? There's always someone else for you to place the blame on instead of taking ownership for your own fucked up actions. I hate to break it to you but it's the truth. The difference being, my mom was too polite to say it to your face, and unlike you all my mom ever wanted was for me to be happy, and for a time I really thought I was with you"

"So be happy. Be happy with me." He pleads, creeping closer, but this time I'm not going to allow him to catch me off guard.

Wiping the fresh stream of tears from my stained face, I stand tall and square my shoulders, preparing myself for another fight. "That's the problem. You don't make me happy, Daniel. Not anymore. You've never seen me as your equal. I'll never be a priority to you... I'll always be an option. Nothing more than an afterthought.

"Emilie, you don't mean that. This is the grief talking."

I shake my head, desperate for him to take me seriously. "No Daniel, I mean every single word so hear me loud and clear when I tell you that we... are... done..." I emphasize each word, hoping that this time he'll listen and take the hint. "There's nothing left for us anymore."

Stepping to the side I move away from him. "I swear, if you walk away from me then there's no going back." he warns me. "If you turn around and leave me here then you'll have no one. Is that really what you want?"

Daniel knows he's losing me and he'll try anything to keep the control over me he once had. He's shooting his last shot, trying to gaslight and manipulate me into staying with him, but his games aren't going to work. Not this time.

"You see..." I say, boring my eyes into his, hopefully for the last time. "That's the difference between you and me. I don't need anyone. I know my own worth and I'm more than capable of doing life by myself. As of next week, I'll be gone. I'll be nothing more than a distant memory. I'll be out of Clearwater for good, and there's nothing you can say or do to change my decision."

With one final look at my mom's grave I say a silent goodbye, more than ready to walk away from Daniel for the last time. Thankfully he doesn't try to stop me as I open the door and climb inside my truck. I don't hesitate as I roll the engine and slam my foot down on the gas, eager to put Daniel and today's events behind me.

That son of a bitch has a bad habit of ruining everything for me, including my last goodbye with my mom.

4

Emilie

I don't stop, tearing through town and miraculously I avoid every stop light as I make my way to Benny's. Skylar had left me a couple of messages during my showdown with Daniel, letting me know that she was waiting for me back at the house. I can't face going back there. Not yet.

If I'm being honest with myself, I don't think I'll ever be ready to go back there. What was once a home is now an empty shell filled with endless memories. Some good, some bad. Constant reminders of what was and what should have been. My head can't handle that so if I can put it off for as long as possible then that's what I'm going to do.

The sun begins to set, saying goodbye to another day as I exit the dirt trail which leads to Benny's. I'm not surprised to find Skylar waiting for me by the doors as I turn into the parking lot and it makes me realize I'm going to miss her so fucking much.

Parking up, I pull down my visor and check my reflection, not sure what kind of hot mess is about to grace my vision. Bloodshot, tearstained eyes look back at me, but I'm a girl who lives for silver linings, and seeing how my new mascara stood the test of time makes me feel a little more put together. It might be small, but I have to find something to be grateful for in this epic shitfest I'm currently living through. My lips haven't fared as well. They're dry and a deep crimson red, no doubt from the constant assault from the bitter winds back at the graveyard.

I wish I could try to find the energy to care, but I'm done. I have nothing left. I'm surprised I'm still functioning after the events of today but the low thrum of adrenaline still seeping through my body keeps me going.

"How did it go?" Skylar asks as I approach her, my black boots crunching on the gravel beneath my feet. Her wide eyes and folded arms tell me she's been worried about me. I can't blame her because if the roles were reversed then I'd be worrying about her too.

Biting down on my bottom lip, worrying it between my teeth I think on what to say to her. I'm exhausted. I'm so tired I can feel it deep in my bones and I don't know if I'll be able to survive another back and forth. I can't keep the situation with Daniel from her though. That's friend code 101.

"I had some time," I confess, deciding to keep it straight to the point. "Nowhere near as much as I'd like, but I'm just thankful it was peaceful for the most part."

I push the door open and step inside Benny's Bar and Grill, grateful for the warmth on my face. I didn't realize how cold I was but I suppose that's what shock does to you. With each step I can hear Skylar screaming at me inside her head, desperate for me to elaborate but I keep my mouth closed, forcing one foot in front of the other; heading straight to our usual seats by the far wall. Out of sight, out of mind... just the way I like it.

No sooner has my frozen ass touched down on the pleather, she's on me. "Erm... excuse me, but you're gonna need to tell me what you meant when you said, *'for the most part...'*."

Puffing out my cheeks, I shrug back at her as she reaches out and pulls a menu from the holder even though she's ordered the same meal for years. "It's nothing."

"Something happened and you're going to tell me." she pushes, not ready to back down.

I knew this would happen. Skylar has always been able to see straight through me. I decide it's best to get this over with anyway. I love Skylar with a passion, but she's like a dog with a bone when she's zoned in on something. My life is no exception.

"Daniel happened." There, I said it, and now I need to wait for the inevitable onslaught.

"No fucking way..." her hand slams down on the table, her eyes growing wide and she doesn't try to hide her excitement that she's about to get the tea. If there's drama then you can bet your ass that Sky wants to be in the know, even if it is at my expense. But like they say, there's no secrets between friends. "I can't believe he actually had the balls to turn up."

"Well, believe it because it happened."

"What did he want?"

Licking my dry lips, I reach out and take a look at my own menu, more to busy my hands and forcing my emotions onto something else. "I'm not really sure, but it wasn't for small talk like he's tried to make out." My eyes scan the menu but everything is a blur as fresh tears threaten to spill over. No fucking way am I going to shed another tear for that stupid, heartless boy. "But you know Daniel, he loves nothing more than to cause a scene and make everything about him. He tried to convince me to stay with him, but I think we both know that's a no go. Either that or he's ran up another huge debt with his dealer and wanted to ask me for another loan that I'll never get back."

"Anything is possible with that freak." I think it's fair to say that Skylar has never been Daniel's biggest fan and now that I'm out of his wicked clutches I'm starting to see why so many people hated him. "I'd bet he's ran up another debt expecting you to bail him out as usual."

"Probably," I admit. "But he isn't my problem anymore."

"Fuck... I knew I should have stayed with you. Like you've not had enough to deal with today."

I smile at my best friend, forever grateful to have her on my side. "Honestly, I don't think it would have made much of a difference. Knowing Daniel, he was probably hiding out in the shadows waiting for you to leave. He's always been too chicken shit to make his move in public." Daniel has always preferred to attack me behind closed doors. That way he knew he'd be wearing me down while making me become dependent on him.

"Nothing changes then." Skylar muses as she offers me a small encouraging smile and even though I feel terrible, I can't stop myself from returning it.

"Nope. But if there's anything good to come out of this mess then it's knowing I won't have to deal with him or his bullshit for much longer."

A small silence fills the space between us before Skylar's lips part, the realization of my confession hitting her slowly. "You've made your mind up then?" Her voice is small, uneasy at the thought of being without me and I feel the same. I don't want to leave her. Never in a million years but right now I can't see any other way.

"I hadn't decided. Not really." I admit. "At least not until Daniel made an unwelcome appearance. Just seeing him there next to my mom's grave, it made me realize that tomorrow isn't promised to anyone. He made me realize that Clearwater isn't for me... at least not right now."

"Gee... thanks, babe. You sure know how to make a girl feel loved."

"No," I shake my head, trying to make her understand where I'm coming from. "You mean everything to me. You know you do, it's just... I don't know. It's hard to explain." My head is all over the place and I'm struggling to process my own thoughts. "I think the change will be good for me. It might even give me a chance to process everything that's happened. Maybe allow me to try to get my head around it all."

Skylar doesn't say anything for a few moments as she watches me. Finally, after what feels like a lifetime she breaks it. "It makes sense, I suppose." she nods back at me but I can tell she's upset that I'm leaving town. I'm upset too. I don't even know how I'm supposed to function without her. We've been best friends ever since she stormed into my life back in first grade and demanded that I be her best friend, and I haven't been able to get rid of her since. Not that I'd want to. Skylar is everything I could have ever wished for in a best friend. She's a solid part of me. Now and forever.

"It wasn't an easy decision, Sky." I promise.

"I know. I just hate that you're having to deal with that splat of sperm on top of everything else."

I lean back into the seat and shrug my shoulders, trying to shield my emotions as best I can. "Daniel was always going to be a problem. You and I both know it was going to happen at some point. He was desperate to drag me down to his level. More than happy to take advantage of my vulnerability for his own sick and twisted games. The sooner I get away from him the better."

Without a beat, Skylar reaches across the table and takes my hand in hers, squeezing a little reassurance back into me. "I've got you no matter what you decide or where you go. And if it doesn't work out then you've always got a home here with me."

"Oh yeah... because your mom is going to love having another mouth to feed."

"My mom should have thought about keeping her legs closed."

"Sky, you can't say shit like that." I scold, hoping that she's joking.

"Sure I can. Plus, my mom loves you and you know it. She'd never see you go without." It's true. Skylar's mom has always made me feel welcome and part of the family. I'd go as far to say she's been like a second mom to me over the years and I know she'd put me up in a heartbeat if that's what I wanted. I'd love to stay, but it's just not logical right now. Especially after she welcomed twins into the fold two months ago. She didn't even know she was pregnant until she doubled over in the bathroom and shocked us all when she gave birth there and then to two healthy little girls. Or the crotch goblins as Skylar likes to call them. She really adores them. I think it's just going to take her a while to adjust. To accept that she's no longer an only child and the apple of her mom's eye.

"So, have you decided where you're going to go?"

"Sarah called and said I could fly over to hers anytime I wanted. Then Nathan called and said he'd like me to stay with him."

"Wait... Nathan? Nathan as in your dad. The man who's acted like you didn't exist for the past eighteen years. I hope you took Sarah up on that trip to England and secured me tickets too."

Pursing my lips I close my eyes, knowing she isn't going to be happy with my answer.

"You didn't. You did not sack off a trip to England to stay with a man who was basically an additional ingredient when your mom cooked you up for nine months."

"It's closer to you." I try to plead my case knowing full well it's fucking crazy.

"Am I missing something here?" Skylar has never been one to hold back. She's always been one to tell people exactly what's on her mind. It's one of the reasons I love her, and now she's confirming what I already know. I've lost the fucking plot.

"See, this is why I didn't want to say anything yet. I need a change and a change is as good as any, and this way I can still see you."

"But he doesn't know the first thing about you, Em. It will be like living with a total stranger, and if you want my opinion, I don't think you're in the right headspace to be dealing with something so full on."

I know she means well and I appreciate it, but I know deep down I have to do this. "That's exactly why I'm doing it. I need something to take my mind off my mom. I need a fresh start and maybe staying with Nathan will be the distraction I need. I just need to contact him and let him know."

5

Emilie

I thought about phoning Nathan, but I quickly decided against it when I realized how awkward it would be. Granted, not as awkward as living with him, but I'll cross that bridge when it comes to it. We haven't spoken and up until last week I always assumed that's how it would stay.

Obviously, he'd heard along the grapevine that my mom had passed. The rumor mill is shameless even if you're not involved in someone's life. As far as I could tell there wasn't any love lost between my mom and dad, but there must have been a little something there for him to even think about reaching out. Maybe he's your typical male and his ego couldn't handle people thinking badly of him so he needed to make sure he took on the responsibilities of caring for his child. A child he's not bothered with for eighteen years.

It's highly unlikely but I'm also aware that there are always two sides to a story and maybe he had his reasons to abandon me. Maybe my mom decided it was for the best that we had no contact.

What the fuck am I doing even contemplating moving to someone's house. A person I've never met but who also shares half of my DNA. I knew I'd lost it. I just didn't realize just how much.

I'd like to make it clear that this man; Nathan, doesn't mean jackshit to me. I'm not on some kind of mission to replace my mom. I'd be more than happy to carry on living my life without ever seeing him, but the option to move in with him. A different life where no one knows me was on the table and I know deep down I'd be a fool not to take it.

The offer wasn't going away and without realizing it Daniel pushed me into the waiting arms of another male who had let me down. The difference being I don't have any emotional ties to Nathan. Unlike my cheating scumbag of an ex. It's funny because Daniel is the one who made the decision for me, and now it's starting to feel right. Like I was supposed to be put on this path all along.

A small part of me thought I'd feel different when I woke up this morning. That I might have fixed my broken mind and built up some sense while I slept, but surprisingly the move still seems to be on the cards and I can feel the small sparks of excitement festering deep in my stomach. I can try to overlook the fact I'll be living with a man who didn't want me or any part in my life, but so long as I focus on why I want to move out of Clearwater I'm sure I'll be fine.

I'd be a fool to miss out on this fresh start. The perfect opportunity to build a new me while I try to push through and navigate my grief. I don't need a relationship with Nathan, and I hope he isn't expecting one in return because the only parent who truly mattered to me is gone, and she's not coming back.

Life is short and all of this has made me realize I need to live my life. I need to seize all the chances and risks thrown my way because I'm the one who's still living and breathing. Everyday is a gift and I don't plan on wasting a single one.

My blood ran cold when I opened Nathan's polite but rather formal email. At first I felt violently sick at the thought of speaking to him. I mean come on, how fucked up is that he actually went out of his way to reach out to me. It almost felt like he was trying to use my mom's untimely death as a way to build bridges with me. That is not going to happen. We didn't have a bridge to begin with. He burned that long ago with my mom and it turned to ash. I don't think any kind of relationship can survive that level of trauma.

I had every intention of ignoring his email. Initially I was hellbent on staying in Clearwater. This place has been my home for a long time and I wanted to make it work, but then that self-centered son of a bitch turned up and put the final nail in the coffin. Pun totally intended.

Aside from Skylar, there's nothing left here for me anymore. No mom. No home. No deadbeat boyfriend. The bottom line is, my mom shouldn't have died, period. She was thirty-nine for fucks sake. She was in her prime. All of her best years were still ahead of her and now in a cruel twist of fate, she doesn't get to experience a single one. That's why I'm determined to up and leave. I need to make something of myself. I need to find a way to make my mom proud. I made a promise to her this morning that I'm going to do everything I can to live my life, take every opportunity so she can see it through my eyes.

I never thought I'd be saying this but starting over never felt so good.

6

Emilie

"Hello."

She answers on the third ring, her voice hoarse and dry like she's not stopped crying.

"Sarah, hey. It's me, Emilie." I walk across the kitchen toward the misted window and switch on the light. Even during the day, the house feels dark and heavy—full of stagnant energy.

"Hey beautiful." I hear her smile down the line, her mood lifting significantly. "It's so good to hear from you. How have you been holding up?"

"Oh, you know..." Numb. Empty. Questioning my life at every turn. "I'm trying to take each day as it comes, but I'll be honest. It's all blurring into one big fuck up."

"Oh, baby... I know exactly what you mean. Listen, I'm so sorry I wasn't there by your side yesterday..."

"You don't need to apologize. Skylar was with me, plus mom didn't want you to travel. I've always respected your decisions."

Sarah has been my mom's best friend since they were little kids. Much like me and Skylar; and the irony isn't lost on me. I know she'll be hurting and riddled with so much guilt but my mom made it perfectly clear that she didn't want Sarah flying back home while she's experiencing a high-risk pregnancy. Plus, my mom said she didn't want a goodbye, more of a see you later. She was adamant that she'd be with her wherever she was in the world and it wasn't worth putting them both at risk. It's fair to say that Sarah wasn't happy with my mom telling her what she should and shouldn't be doing, but she respected her wish. I mean, how could anyone argue with their best friend's dying wish?

To be honest, I was a little surprised she listened. Doing as she's told isn't Sarah's strong point and it used to get her into a lot of trouble until she settled down with Morgan. I'm sure if my head had been more conscious of my surroundings, I would have expected her to jump out from behind the church or something.

Sarah's always been bat shit crazy and a little on the reckless side. I see so much Skylar in her. Like Sky, she's always been a constant in my life. Hell, she was even in the delivery room as my mom's birthing partner because my dad was nowhere to be seen. He disappeared when he realized I was a spill he couldn't afford to clean up.

His loss.

Thankfully I don't have any daddy issues. I never needed him. My mom made sure I had everything I needed and more growing up. She made sure I couldn't miss what I never had.

My aunt Sarah though; she struggled to have kids of her own. She tried naturally and multiple rounds of IVF but it wasn't meant to be. She didn't allow that to deter her in her mission of becoming a mum and giving back to society. After moving to England, she started fostering troubled and neglected kids. Watching kids struggle is a massive hard no for her so she makes sure they have a stable home along with everything else they could possibly need, even if the ungrateful fucks treat her like shit most of the time.

And then as if by some miracle she fell pregnant naturally and she's due on Christmas Eve. Before my mom's death I believed the world worked in mysterious ways. Now, although I still hold onto a little hope of that being true, I've decided it likes to have fun when it comes to fucking up my life, but we roll.

She was the first to offer me a place to stay. The thought of packing up and moving to England was scary but also exciting but it's just too far away for me. Hollow Heights on the other hand is only an hour's drive away.

Confessing in hospital, my mom told me should anything happen to her sooner rather than later then she'd love for me to spend time with Nathan. Something I struggled to get my head around for the longest time. Until now.

I'm guessing my mom must have loved him at one point. Maybe she hoped I'd get to know him and see for myself if he had any redeeming qualities about him, however my mom was a good judge of character so I'm not about to hold my breath.

"So, have you made a decision about the move yet?" She asks, pulling me out of my thoughts, catapulting me straight back into my personal hell. "I know it's still early days and I want you to know there's absolutely no pressure for you to move anywhere you don't want to. None whatsoever."

"Thanks." This is why Sarah is one in a million. This is a woman who is heavily pregnant, raising wannabe gangsters. Someone who's just lost her best friend and she's still looking out for everyone else. "I've been thinking about it a lot actually" I confess before dropping my weary body down onto the sofa.

"Sounds promising." She teases. She doesn't try to hide her surprise as her voice raises a few extra notches.

"I promise it isn't. I know it's going to sound hella crazy but I've decided to go stay at Nathan's for a while. It's still close to Sky and you're gonna have a crazy Christmas as it is." Confessing my decision out loud means I can't go back on it.

"I'm glad you listened to your mom but I can't say I envy you, kid. It's going to be one long and strange road you're about to go down."

"You and I both, huh."

"Squeezing a baby out of my cooch will be a breeze."

"I'm going to take your word for it." I laugh my first genuine laugh in weeks and it feels so good. "But I think it will do us both good to have something to look forward to."

"That's my girl. Your mom was so proud of you, you know."

"Hopefully I don't let her down when I go to live with the added yeast."

"The added what?"

"Just something Sky said."

"Then tell me no more." Her small laugh filters down the line and I really wish my mom was here with us. "But just remember that if it doesn't work out with the *added yeast* then you always have a home here with me."

My chest swells, filled with nothing but love for the other half who raised me. It means so much that she still wants to look out for me.

"I know and I'll keep that in mind. England sounds great and all but it doesn't have a Skylar. Nathan's what, two towns over?" All this time and he could have driven to see me if he really wanted to, but like the true coward he is, the bastard didn't do shit.

"When do you leave?"

"Monday." I sigh, a part of me regretting my decision, but it's too late to back out now. "That gives me plenty of time to pack up here with a few days spare to get my shit together."

"Don't put too much pressure on yourself. I'm going to tell you exactly what I used to tell your mom: take it one day at a time and see where it takes you."

"Thanks Sarah."

"Anytime. Just promise me one thing…"

"Shoot…"

"Go easy on Nathan. He wasn't always a self-centered asshole. Boys just have a habit of refusing to grow up. And remember, if it doesn't work out, I'll pay for a one-way flight to England. For you and Sky."

"Bet. I'm gonna have to go but I promise I'll check in with you once I'm settled."

"Make sure you do. Now go and show the world what Emilie Garcia is made of. I'll be the one screaming loudest from the sidelines."

7

Emilie

I needed to get out of the house and fast before the walls started to cave in. There's only so many times I can look at the same walls before I can't think straight. My chest was getting tighter, making it harder to breathe as the grief rolled in, barreling into me like a tsunami, crashing into my chest and stealing all the air from my lungs.

The sooner I'm out of this town, the better. There's just too many memories here.

"Earth to Emilie..." Skylar shouts, waving her hands in front of my face to get my attention.

"Shit, I zoned out, didn't I?"

"Only for a solid ten minutes or so but don't worry, I already ordered for you."

"Thanks. I seriously don't know what I'm going to do without you."

"So don't leave Clearwater. Stay here with me."

"Trust me, if I thought that was the best decision for me, I'd stay in a heartbeat, but something's telling me that I need to do this. That it's time for me to put the last few months behind me. I can't explain it. All I know is in my head it makes sense."

"Well, I'm not gonna sit here and pretend I'm not gutted because I am." She pouts back at me, her brown curly hair falling down around her shoulders. "But I know you have to do whatever it is you need to do."

"Have I told you that I'm going to miss the fuck out of you?" I whisper, once again battling against the quiver of emotions in my voice. Whether I want to admit it or not, this is happening and our days together are numbered, and as much as it pains me to leave her, I know I have to do this.

"I'm gonna miss the fuck out of you too, bitch." she replies without skipping a beat. "But it doesn't have to be forever, right?"

"Right," I smile, my heart swelling a little more. "I'm going to give it a year with Nathan and see how I feel."

"A year?" She exclaims, jumping out of her seat and almost choking on her soda.

"What, did you think I was packing up just for a two-week vay-cay?"

"Obviously not," she pouts some more, "but your girl was living in hope, that's all."

Shaking my head, I worry my bottom lip between my teeth, "I hate this." I tell her truthfully and I mean every word.

"What if I told you there could be a way for you to make it up to me?" Leaning forward I can't miss the dangerous glint in her eyes. A look I've seen many times before and none have ended all too well for us.

We're seated in our usual booth at Benny's. "Hmmm, I'm not sure I like the sound of where this is headed…" I tell her, twirling my straw around the glass.

"It will be fun" Her smile widens as she tries to sell me her plan. "Hear me out before you make any rash decisions."

I hold my hands up in surrender as I give in. "Okay, I'm all ears."

"Perfect." Clapping her hands together she looks like all her christmases have come at once. "You've been after a change of scenery, right?"

"Right."

"You need a little something to take your mind away from all the bullshit and pain..."

"Correct." I have no idea where she's going with this but I already promised I'd listen so I have no choice but to press my lips together and hear her out. I have to uphold my side of the deal.

"And... It's Halloween this weekend."

"Nope." I say instantly, popping the P for added effect while shaking my head vigorously, her plan already taking form in my mind. "It's not happening, Sky."

"Oh, come on." She pleads with me and I know she isn't beneath begging, even if she is in public. "It will be fun and it's exactly what you need. Plus, you know we've wanted to do this for ages."

"Sure, it probably will be fun, but I'm not feeling it at the moment."

"No, you think you're not feeling it, but we both know that's a load of bull."

"I swear. I promise I'm not being a bore. I just don't think I'd enjoy it."

"Fuck off. We're talking about a weekend away here."

"Exactly. I'm not in the right headspace, Sky. I appreciate what you're trying to do, but I'm not feeling it."

Leaning forward, Skylar means business as she challenges me, her eyes dancing with a mixture of danger and excitement. This girl is refusing to take no for an answer and she's just going to keep pushing until she breaks me down and I'm left with no other option than to give in. "Have you looked at it another way and thought that this might be exactly what you need? It's the perfect place to escape reality. A chance for you to kick back, relax and let your hair down while you still can. God knows you're going to need it before you go and live with the sperm donor who didn't even want to donate."

"Okay, calm down. You're getting a little personal there, Sky."

She watches me in silence as I process her plan slowly, more to make her sweat as she waits not so patiently for my response. Skylar knows what she's doing. She's trying to sell me the weekend of a lifetime and minute by minute she's already wearing me down.

"Just picture the scene..." she continues, refusing to let up, waving her hands around before leaning closer over the table, her brown eyes wide and expectant. "A weekend away, secluded in a cabin somewhere in Hollow Heights... at Halloween." She winks at me, knowing she's selling it to my soul. "I know all about those smutty romance books that you read when you think no one is looking. I know what happens in them too."

"And your point?"

"My point is go ahead and tell me what's not to enjoy." Waggling her brows at me she knows she has me hook, line and sinker.

"Fine, I'll admit it sounds amazing..." I'm caving just like she knew I would. "But I have so much to do and not much time."

"Babe, you know you're not alone, right?"

"Of course I do."

"Good. Because I'll be helping you pack. I'll even wave you off while my heart breaks before your eyes as you leave me. I'll allow you to see that vulnerable side I hide so well. All I ask is that we do one last fun thing together before you leave me all alone in this hell hole."

"Fine. You win." I say reluctantly. "But don't you dare say I never do anything for you."

8

Emilie

"I cannot believe I agreed to this." I mutter under my breath as I climb out of my truck. We're in the middle of fucking nowhere and I lost signal on my phone a few miles back.

"Well, get used to it because we're here and we're going to have fun." Skylar tells me firmly as she walks around the truck before popping the boot, pulling out some of our supplies.

I really wished I shared her enthusiasm, but I'm beginning to regret my decision with each moment that passes.

"It's Devil's night, baby. Hopefully he'll be on our side and bless our unyielding loyalty to his cause by rewarding us with some sexy as fuck masked men ready to entertain us and chase us through the woods to make this weekend even more memorable."

I roll my eyes at my best friend. Just when I thought she couldn't shock me anymore she always manages to pull something else out of the bag. "I hate to be the one to break it to you," I say as I cast my curious gaze around the woodland and find we're completely sealed from the outside world, shielded by endless towering trees and dense woodland. "But it looks like it's just the two of us out here."

"For now." she beams back at me, a mystical glint shimmering in her eyes as she walks past me, like she knows something I don't.

"Sky, this place is deserted."

"Of course, because that's how it's supposed to feel. It all adds to the illusion. It adds a bit of thrill to the unexpected. After all, no one gets attacked unless they're alone, right."

"We're not going to get attacked because there's no one else here." I say again and this time I get a cold shiver down my spine and all the small hairs on the back of my neck stand tall; a warning that all isn't as it seems.

"Oh, there are others." Skylar tells me confidently. "We meet by the firepit at seven."

Great. I guess I should be happy that one of us knows what's happening. After all, I'm just here to hold up my side of the bargain. Not because I want to be.

Without another word I follow behind her as she approaches the small, wooden cabin. On first look it's cozy and quaint. The wooden walls are damp and covered in moss. Telltale signs of weathering many storms.

This place is so quiet and if it wasn't eerie as fuck, I'd say it could be peaceful. The only sound around us is the fallen leaves rustling below our feet.

Stepping around Sky, I reach for the handle on the oak door as her hands are full and another shiver runs down my spine, making me feel a little on edge. I look over my shoulder and scan my eyes on the trees, I get the strong sensation that somebody is watching us. I'm being stupid. I'm just tired and my mind is on overdrive. I shrug it off and push the thought to the back of my mind. Nobody even knows we're here.

Flicking on the lights I step back and allow Skylar to move past me before quickly shutting the door. Just to be on the safe side. Fuck. We're in the middle of the woods. How the fuck are we supposed to be safe?

Skylar turns and smiles at me, beaming like the sun as she says, "the hunt starts tonight and I am so fucking here for it."

9

Emilie

"Have you ever thought about being chased down by a masked man hidden deep in the woods?"

"No." I lie effortlessly, "but something tells me that you have, and often."

Skylar has always been open and honest about her sexuality and endless desires. She's comfortable in her body and she's confident when it comes to what she wants.

Me, I'm more on the quieter side. A little more reserved, choosing to voice my wants and needs silently, inside my head. No doubt the way Daniel conditioned me and made me feel. My mind instantly catapults back to the night my mom died, making me question Skylar's current motives.

I didn't want to be all alone in an empty house. My emotions were all over the place and before we knew it, we were drinking our emotions. Lonely, vulnerable and neglected by Daniel, one thing led to another and before too long Skylar and I were finding comfort in each other. We crossed the friendship line one too many times that night.

We did things to each other that we had no business doing. Did I regret it? Not one bit. In all honesty, it activated a new side to me. Opening up my hidden desires and pushing them to the surface. Not that I'd ever feel comfortable admitting that out loud.

Before I can stop them, vivid images from that night crash to the forefront of my mind and I remember everything.

We've never discussed it, but my body remembers every stolen touch, each delicate stroke of our tongues and fingers, and every soft kiss we impaled on each other. My core clenches at the memories.

Is this why Skylar has decided to bring me out here? To get me all alone in the woods? I doubt it. I know Skylar well enough to know that if she wanted a repeat of that night then she wouldn't need to drag me somewhere secluded to achieve it. No... my mind is telling me she has something else, something more fucked up hidden up her sleeve.

I'm still new to exploring my body, and anyone else's for that matter. Sure, Daniel and I played around every now and again. We lost ourselves to a little heavy petting here and there, but that's about it. We never moved past second base and if he came in his pants then he was a happy camper. Sex always seemed to be off the table with him so I gave up pressing on the subject.

But that night me and Skylar lost ourselves and found comfort in each other, it was something else. I can't even find the words to describe it.

"Hmmm... something tells me you're a lying bitch. Don't forget I know you better than anyone and I've witnessed that dark side of yours."

I feel the heat of my arousal from that night rush to my cheeks and I'm grateful that it's dark out.

Skylar laughs when I don't say anything, the soft crunch beneath our feet the only sound as she leads us down the narrow dirt path, towards our destination.

The trees grow sparse, narrowing before they give way to a small opening, leading to a barren meadow. It looks empty except for a blazing fire in the middle. As we edge closer, I realize that Skylar was right after all and we're not alone.

Four hooded figures sit around the fire-pit, and they sit in total silence. Each one is dressed in a black cloak, disguised to perfection under the haunted night sky, concealing their true identities.

"What the hell is this?" I ask, feeling like I'm about to walk to my death. "This doesn't look like a Halloween party to me. It looks more like a sacrifice."

"Hmmm... now doesn't that sound delicious?" She smirks back at me as we move closer, but my footing falters as though she's transporting me straight to the deepest depths of hell where I've been sent to repent for my sins.

"I'm not sure about this..." I confess on a hushed whisper, desperately trying to ignore the heated anticipation and excitement trimming through my veins.

"I promised you fun. I promised you a distraction and that's what you're going to get."

I don't get a chance to say anything else when the hooded figure sitting directly opposite me pushes himself up and stands tall, his large frame casting me and Skylar deep into the shadows.

"Welcome to the Hollows." He bellows, his voice deep and rustic as it echoes out around the meadow and I can feel their hidden but watchful eyes burning into me. "Do you accept the challenge set before you?"

"Challenge?" I question, my brows knitting together in confusion. No one answers me, instead it's Skylar who breaks the silence.

"We do." she replies, her voice loud and clear, oozing a confidence I've never heard before. I don't know what she's gone and caught us up in, but she needs to start talking and fast.

"We do, what?" I bite out, a mixture of fear and excitement prickling my bare flesh and goose pimples appear which I know have nothing to do with the chill in the air.

Skylar eventually tears her eyes away from the hooded figure before us and looks right at me and I see she's smirking. I swear I don't think I've ever seen her look so excited as she does right in this moment.

In my peripheral I see the figure moving toward us, only the firepit between me, Skylar and the four masked strangers. Danger knots deep in my stomach as the realization kicks in. This isn't some innocent Halloween party. No, this is an orchestrated masked man hunt.

"The rules are simple…" The figure states. "Run—but if we catch you, we fuck you."

My mouth falls open at his direct admission. This has to be some kind of joke. A wind up. "What the actual fuck?" I mouth at my best friend and she rewards me with another smile before grabbing my hand and pulling me close as she whispers, "Things are about to get fucked up in the best possible way."

"Do you accept the challenge?" he asks again, and this time I know he's directing his question at me. Skylar squeezes my hand some more and I swallow hard before nodding my head in acceptance. I'm either going to regret this decision for the rest of my life or it's about to become one of the most exciting nights of my life.

I feel all four of them watching me under their hoods. "You have to say it out loud." Skylar whispers.

"Yes, we accept." I say before really thinking about what I've just signed myself up for. Surprising myself at the conviction in my voice.

The main ringleader bows his head as he replies. "Go. The chase begins at midnight."

10

Emilie

"What the fuck, Sky." Is all I manage to say as we approach our cabin.

"What?" She throws her arms up casually, like this is just another everyday occurrence. Maybe for her it is, but me not so much. "You said you wanted a little fun. A way to forget the stress and trauma you've been forced to carry around."

"Yeah... like maybe with a movie or a book."

"But this is so much better than any book. Here you get to live out all those crazy fantasies with zero judgment. One final act of rebellious filth before you leave town."

"Gee, why didn't I think of that? Oh, maybe because this is the town I'm going to be moving to. Anyone could be concealed under those hoods." I remind her.

"They're not from around here." she promises. "I checked it all out when I came across the event. Here, take this," Skylar bats away my worries as she passes me a bottle of Jack and I take it willingly. "I've got a feeling we're going to need it."

We have four hours to prepare and no amount of whiskey could get me ready to be chased by masked strangers through the woods.

Oh well, I guess there's no going back now. I pour us both generous shots in two coffee mugs I found on the counter and place one into Skylar's waiting hand.

"We need a plan."

"How so?" I ask, not sure where her head is at the moment. "Do we even get a choice?" It sure sounded to me like the end goal wasn't debatable to me.

"Of course we don't. We signed up to be captives for the night. We want them to fuck us. That's the end goal, but at the same time we don't want to make it too easy for them. We need to make them work for it."

11

Emilie

I don't have any sense of time when all the electricity blows in the cabin, leaving me and Skylar in total darkness.

"It's time." Skylar claps her hands and her voice floats in the air between us. "Are you ready?"

"Not really." I confess, although the whiskey has made me less uptight. I'm still unable to believe I've decided to go through with this. But it looks like it's too late to change my mind. I wouldn't know where I was headed anyways and I'd probably fall right into one of their deadly traps so it would be nothing more than a pointless and wasted effort on my part.

We leave the cabin in total silence, ready as I'll ever be for this chase. My senses are on high alert. Everything seems heightened out here in the dark. The trees move with the wind, causing elongated shadows under the moonlight, catching me off guard as we creep through the woods.

"I think we'd have a better shot if we split up." Skylar whispers, anxiously taking in her surroundings.

"Are you being serious? Do you want me to fucking die a slow and painful death out here?"

"Only if it's death by orgasm, baby."

"You are so fucked in the head. Do you know that?"

"Yep, and that's why you love me babe."

It feels like I've been creeping around the woods for an eternity. I don't know where I'm going and I know I'm going to be fucked when the hooded guys catch up with me. There's no way I'll be able to outrun them. Not out here in the dark where I've got no sense of awareness.

I jump out of my skin when I hear someone close to me. "Sky..." I whisper. "Sky is that you?"

Nothing but silence greets me.

My heart beats wildly in my chest, the blood rushing to my ears. Fight or flight. Flight wins every single time. Without thinking, I run straight ahead, but I trip, stumbling and falling over an upturned branch before falling into something hard.

"Boo." The voice booms as he brings his masked face to mine. His hood is down, but the authority he possesses oozes out from his every pore. The ringleader of the group. Great. Just what I fucking needed.

"Who are you?" I ask, my body trembling on the floor and I don't expect him to answer me. He's already made it perfectly clear this is his game and we're just the pieces.

His head tilts to the side as he takes me in. "I can be anything you want me to be, Emilie."

"How... how do you know my name?" I stammer. Fuck, is this someone I know? Fear creeps in, talking over my body and festering like the plague. I don't want to play anymore, but I've got a strange feeling that whatever I want doesn't even factor into this deadly game.

He moves closer as I shuffle back, desperate to put some space between us. Stones and branches dig deep into my palms, cutting the flesh but I don't let up—not until my back slams into a solid tree trunk, winding me and knocking all the air from my lungs.

Reaching out, his hand cups my face, his thumb tracing my bottom lip before parting them. "Such a pretty little mouth." he praises me before sliding his thumb deep inside. I bite down without hesitation, my reflexes kicking in. He doesn't remove it, only hisses as he forces it deeper into my mouth, almost cutting off my oxygen supply. I bite down harder, desperate to get him off me, but the psychopath only laughs at my pitiful attempt.

He loosens his grip a little, but only enough so I can breathe before he slides his free hand into the back pocket of his worn black jeans and an audible gasp escapes me when he pulls out a knife.

If I make it out of here alive, I swear I'm going to kill Skylar with my bare fucking hands.

"I can see the fear in your eyes, pup." I can hear the smile beneath his mask as he brings the blade to my throat, pressing the cool metal against my flesh and my body trembles in response.

"You remember the rules?" He asks. I nod, never once taking my eyes away from him. "I catch you; I fuck you."

I nod again as he removes his thumb completely from my mouth.

"I want to hear you say it."

Licking my dry lips, I swallow hard as he pushes the blade deeper forcing me to clear my throat. "You caught me, so now you get to fuck me."

The masked stranger growls out his approval, and he sounds almost primal. A sound which sends a pool of desire rushing to my core. I'm a little scared, but I'm more aroused and I'm not even mad about it.

"Stand." He orders and I willingly obey, totally captivated by his mystery. I'm desperate to know more about him. I stand at full height and he still towers over me, forcing me to tilt my head to look up at him.

His knife slowly travels from my neck, all the way down my chest, slowing at my nipples before coming to a total stop between my thighs.

"I want you to spread them for me like a good little slut."

Once again, my body obeys before juddering when the cold blade glides across my bare pussy. His free hand grips my neck, pushing my head back against the tree and a reckless moan of pleasure falls from my lips.

"Do you like that, pup?" He tightens his grip some more. "You might look all innocent but I can see it in your eyes. You like it rough and I'm more than happy to give you what you want. What you deserve."

I'm speechless. I have no words as he pulls the knife away, leaving me feeling somewhat exposed as he releases me. His hands aren't off me for long though when he grabs my waist, digging his fingers in hard before spinning me around so that my back is toward him. He pulls at my wrists and pulls them behind my back and then another brush of cold metal kisses my skin as he places handcuffs on me.

"Turn back around." He demands. "And open up those legs again. Show me what belongs to me."

No sooner have I done as I'm told, I feel the heat of his hand cup my pussy, causing another growl of appreciation to escape him. I gasp when he removes his hand before forcefully slapping my pussy and it's a heated sensation I could get used to. Before I have a chance to welcome and embrace the pain, he's soothing the sting as he rubs his finger, gliding them over my folds. My breathing falters as he picks up speed and my hips buckle under his touch.

"So wet," he snarls through clenched teeth before sliding his middle finger deep inside me. "So greedy. So perfect and ready to be filled." He adds another finger and I cry out, my body thrumming under his expert touch. How can this stranger know just what I need when I've never known myself?

Fun times were never like this with Daniel.

"Your pussy is desperate for my cock." He's not fucking wrong, but I know better than to open my mouth. Picking up speed he finger fucks me hard and rough, and my hips move as I try to match him thrust for thrust, selfishly chasing my own release as my walls tighten around him.

"Let me see you," I ask before I can stop myself. All of my inhibitions and common sense have well and truly left and I don't think I'll ever get them back. Knowing that I'm close, he withdraws his fingers, denying me of my orgasm before he brings his face close to mine.

"On your knees and open that pretty mouth, nice and wide."

I think about protesting. Refusing to do anything until he's finished me off, but I don't know this guy. He's got a knife and he could easily chop me up into a million pieces if he wanted to. I think it's probably in my best interest to stay silent and keep him on side, at least until I'm reunited with Skylar, whenever that's going to be.

I drop to my knees, feeling the hard and wet debris on the floor, pushing into my knees as I continue to hold my head high. It's a lot harder to remain steady with my hands still cuffed behind my back, and it's even worse when he places a blindfold over my head.

12

Dante

I throw my head back and close my eyes, one hand around her throat and the other fisted in her hair as I fuck her delicate mouth.

The sound of her choking on my cock fuels me, my balls tightening as I thrust harder and faster, chasing my release until I explode inside her, forcing my cock to the back of her throat, holding her head steady so she's forced to swallow every last drop.

I've been waiting for this moment for a while.

I've watched her from afar. We all have. Each one of us holding our own sick and twisted obsession with her.

Who knew that creating a measly event for Halloween would lead her straight to us.

Bringing her straight to the Devil's lair.

13

Emilie

I feel violated. Bruised, swollen and sore, but in all the right ways. My pussy is still throbbing, and I can still feel the delicious assault this wicked stranger has impaled on my innocent body.

I've never felt so wanted or more powerful in my life and we haven't even got around to the main piece of action... *yet.*

Daniel was for real holding out on me, making sure he kept me and my body well and truly hidden from the outside world. Making sure he prevented me from experiencing what fun should actually feel like.

Without a word, my masked captor pulls off my blindfold. He's quite forceful and my head falls back into the tree and when my eyes adjust to the dark, I see his face for the first time and fuck me, I'm not disappointed.

His hair is as black as night as it falls down into his eyes, which are as blue as the ocean. His jaw is sharp and set, his cheekbones chiseled. I swear I've never seen anyone so beautiful and look so dangerous but let me tell you... I'm so fucking here for it. *ALL... OF... IT...*

Whatever this sadistic monster wants to do to me, I'm game. I'll willingly give over my body without question. I guess it's just a shame that I won't see him again once this weekend is over.

My twisted fairytale is ripped from me when his hand grips my shoulder as he pushes me forward, straight through the dense woodland. "What about the handcuffs?" I ask, already knowing that I'm asking too much and pushing my luck. But then if you don't ask you don't get.

"They stay." His voice is authoritative as he walks close behind me. So close I can feel the heat of his breath on the back of my neck and it causes all kinds of sensations to explode in my body.

"But they're hurting me." I moan, hating that I'm showing signs of weakness. He doesn't answer me, instead he pushes me forward with the tip of his blade piercing my flesh above my ass, reminding me that he's the one who holds all the power and I'm the innocent little victim who needs to do as she's told.

"Where are we going?" The question falls from my lips as my curiosity gets the better of me.

"To meet the others." He replies, with zero emotion in his deep rustic voice.

"Others?" It's now that I remember the three other masked men and Skylar hiding somewhere in the woods. I hope she's okay. Maybe they haven't caught her yet, but if one can catch me then the odds are against her with three on her tail.

It doesn't take too long to arrive back at the cabin. Obviously, I mustn't have gone too far to begin with. I walk up the steps, my captor hot on my heels. My wrists, now free, burn as I anxiously open the door to the cabin and my mouth falls open, almost hitting the floor when I take in the scene before me. Like I expected, Skylar didn't win the chase either, only now she has all three of them around her, worshiping her body like she's a goddess.

The knife presses against my skin and I'm forced deeper inside, allowing me to see Skylar tied to the bed, her arms and legs spread wide; granting her captors easy access as they violate her body.

With one cock buried deep in her mouth another one is busy pounding her pussy. She's clearly living her best life right now, and a small part of me envies her.

I watch the hooded figures, still concealed by their masks, mesmerized by the sight before me.

"It looks like the big bad wolf caught you." The third guy says as he approaches me. I open my mouth to answer him but I'm quickly silenced with another jab of the blade as it kisses the base of my spine, pushing me forward toward the bed.

"Be a good little slut and climb on the bed." My very own captor growls, his voice laced with a savage hunger. Moving forward, Skylar's eyes meet mine just as she reaches an earth-shattering orgasm and she reaches out, holding my hand as she rides the wave of her release.

He brings his head close to mine, the heat of his breath tickling my face as he whispers, "I want to watch you play with her." I turn my head to look at him and he rewards me with a wicked grin. "What, it's nothing you haven't done before, pup."

"What…" I stammer out. "How do you…" I begin but a sharp slap on my ass silences me. I have no idea how this stranger can know things about me that only Skylar could know. As expected, he doesn't offer me an answer as he grips my ass and pushes me onto the bed.

I feel all eyes on me as I crawl over to Skylar, lying next to her as she's sprawled out, trying my damned hardest to ignore the delicious predators around us, needing to make sure that she's okay with this.

To be fair, she's being fucked by random masked strangers who chased us through the woods. Something which she'd signed us up for so I'm fairly sure she's going to be okay with me jumping in on the fun. I'll be honest, looking at her right now she looks so fucking hot… hotter than the night we spent together. The smell of sex in the air adds to my arousal and I know Skylar doesn't miss it as she smiles back at me.

A loud rip tears through the room and when I look down, I see that my playsuit has been destroyed. One half on the bed and the other half is already in a pile on the floor. When I look back at the ringleader, I see him smirking back at me, waving his knife proudly in his hand.

"It was getting in the way and I'm not a man who has a lot of patience." He bites out through clenched teeth.

I decide against arguing with him as he moves forward and spreads my legs wide open, giving himself perfect access to my body. I lay back, waiting for him to deliver another delicious assault on my body as Skylar's soft pleasurable moans fill the air around us. The guy who was fucking her mouth changes position, moving to the bottom of the bed and flipping her over in one fluid motion so she's on all fours, before spreading her ass cheeks wide.

"Are you having fun?" She asks just before she screams out in pleasure when the guy at her ass slams his solid cock into her and a rush of desire pools at my core, my pussy throbbing, desperate to be touched while it seems Skylar has all the fun.

I don't get a chance to say anything when the dark and dangerous devil in disguise buries his head between my thighs, his fingers sliding deep inside my pussy before his tongue licks and sucks my clit. My body responds to his touch instantly, shuddering with a heated pleasure as my hips rock back and forth, desperate for more of him, and this time he doesn't let up. A shadow clouds my vision as one of the other masked figures kneels down, his hands cupping my breasts, before sucking my nipple into his heated mouth. I have never been more turned on in my life and my moans are soon matching Skylar's pants next to me.

I feel another orgasm crash through my body before my captor removes his fingers from my wet and swollen pussy, but he doesn't give me any time to recover before he stands, lining his cock up at my entrance. Without any warning, he slams into me, refusing to go slow, or to allow me to adjust to his large length. I open for him willingly as he stretches me and I feel a sense of fullness as he fills me completely. Hands digging into my hips he slams himself deep inside me before pulling his unforgiving length out slowly before slamming straight back into me again. I can't breathe as he pounds me over and over again, my head falling back as I ride out the wave before he stills and I feel the heat of his cum exploding inside of me, his cock throbbing violently inside me.

I don't know what kind of black magic this is but it's a kind of magic that Daniel could only ever dream of. As I try to catch my breath, desperate to regulate my breathing I know my reprieve won't last long from these hungry men. I know this is only the start of a wonderful and wicked weekend hidden deep in the woods with nothing but my best friend and four sinful and sexy masked men for company... and I am so here for it.

Skylar was right. This is a Halloween I'm never going to forget.

14

Emilie

Our secrets will stay locked away in that cabin deep in the woods

What passed by at the weekend was a one-off, and I think me and Skylar can both agree that it's highly unlikely we'll ever see them again. I'll admit, I don't know whether that makes me happy or sad.

I hear my belongings, well what little I've brought, bang around in the back of my truck as I find myself driving back through the Hollows. A reminder of what occurred and my cheeks flush as the heat of my arousal convulses through my body once more.

Hopefully Nathan isn't home so I can spend some much-needed time with my battery-operated boyfriend while reliving and fantasizing about the four masked men who violated my body in the most delicious yet derogatory ways.

It was fucked up for sure.

Would I do it again? Damn fucking straight I would. In one weekend, I've gone from a shy, innocent-ish girl to a sex-obsessed animal... all because of Devil's night and that wicked hunt.

However, I'll store it away as a personal memory. A once in a lifetime experience, but now I need to put it all behind me as I try to focus on the next chapter of my life. However, there's no denying that that night in the woods has changed me. I just don't think it's changed me for the better.

I turn on my wipers as the rain starts to fall before I pull into the large posh house. Obviously, Nathan has been living it up over the years while my mom struggled to make ends meet most of the time.

I kill the engine and decide to leave my belongings in the truck. Nathan hasn't done shit for me over the past eighteen years so collecting my things is the least he can do.

I lift the large knocker and bang it against the door to signal my arrival, but nothing happens. I guess I shouldn't be surprised that Nathan isn't home to greet me. I mean why would he decide to go and break the habit of a lifetime now?

This was a bad idea. I shouldn't have come here. I was stupid to think I could try to make a fresh start here.

I turn to leave as the door opens and when I look back my blood runs cold. All too familiar blue eyes look back at me. His lips tug at the edges, curling into a sadistic smile as he says, "Welcome home, pup. We've been waiting for you."

Kings of Destruction

Are you ready to find out what happens with Emilie and her masked men?

Pre-Order your copy today:

books2read.com/kingsofdestruction1

Have you met the Savage Brothers yet?

Prologue

CALEB

A sense of power and control surge through me. Charging my veins. Making my hollow heart pump steady in my chest, pounding wild and free as I watch the brat spread out before me.

Flat out.

Dead to the fucking world. She's weak. Vulnerable. Trapped and held at the hands of my mercy. Fuck, she's so beautiful. More so when she's like this... utterly defenseless. Comatose; fueling my sadistic need for more. *Always more.*

This isn't my first time. I've been here many times before. Hiding out in her room. Watching silently from the shadows. Slowly creeping closer. Desperate to strike. My intent is to kill her, to watch her bleed out before me, but she's been holding me captive. Gripped by the fucking balls, like a moth drawn to a heated flame. Hypnotized. Knocked completely off guard by the foreign emotions she stirs up inside me.

Emotions I never knew existed—until her.

All I know is that they're unwanted. Unwelcome. Much like her fucking presence in my life.

Her shallow breathing fills the small space between us. Each one more labored than the last. The thrill of not knowing if these will be her final ones keeps me hooked. Focused. A sick and twisted pleasure swells in my chest... as well as my dick at the possibility that tonight's deadly dose could be the lethal shot, sending the electrical current in her heart spiraling out of control, causing her to arrest beneath me.

Wouldn't that be something?

Her life is in my hands and the dumb bitch doesn't even realize it. Too dumb. Too fucking deluded to notice the dangers which surround her every minute of every day. This brat is more than happy to remain deep inside her deluded little bubble, ebbing and flowing along with the invisible yet destructive tides of her captivity.

Playing numb, hiding from her own demons is what she does best. The similarities between us aren't lost on me, no matter how hard I try to ignore them. However, the sweetest part of our situationship is that it's purely one-sided. It doesn't matter what happens between us in this room; both of us blanketed by the darkness because she won't remember. This sleeping beauty won't remember shit. Not a goddamn thing. The sedatives I slip into her water each night make sure of that.

What should have been a routine job; a quick expose and dispose fast turned into something else. Something none of us saw coming, and nothing could have prepared me for the events that followed.

A sick, sadistic obsession.

An obsession I'm not ready to give up on just yet. A secret that only the three of us know. A secret—a sacred vow, which needs to stay between me and my brothers.

We share her.

All of her. Our delicious little victim. The three of us savage her body like she's a piece of meat. Hungry predators tearing her apart. This brat: our little fuck piece loves every fucking moment we impale on her small, perfect, forbidden body.

Our captive has been conditioned to think our sadistic and psychotic behavior is normal. A little wild and crazy, but normal all the same. An act of lust. A vicious, selfish need while fooling her mind into thinking we care about her. This stupid damsel is adamant she can change us. That she can tame the wicked Savage brothers. But that isn't possible. Even if there wasn't a nasty history which binds us, you can't physically love someone with a hollow heart. You can't change what has already been made.

No, the truth of her captivity is far more hideous. More damaging and destructive than she could ever comprehend. What she doesn't know is that she's an integral part of us... but not in the way she wants to be. It's kinda funny how life works out. Especially when this disobedient brat has always been the missing piece to the deadly and destructive puzzle we've been trying to solve. One I've spent many years working on, silently watching from afar... and now, thanks to a wonderful twist of fate, this damsel in distress is mine. She belongs to me. My brothers can do with her as they wish, but she's mine to fuck up in the best possible way.

My revenge is getting close. So close that I can almost taste the sweet victory from her hot salty tears.

Hell, if only that were the case. That's how it used to be. How it fucking should be but all my plans, every single one went straight out the window when I came face to face with her for the first time. I fucking hated how she made me *feel*. I'm notorious for being brutal. For being an emotionless bastard but fuck if she didn't break something in me. I'd gone from being super confident in my decisions to second guessing myself at every turn.

I knew I had to change things. I had to mix things up and fast. If my game plan was going to happen the way I needed it to, then I needed to work smarter, not harder. I needed to use everything to my advantage. Every minute detail—every step of mass destruction had to be timed to perfection.

No one was more shocked than me to find out just how much I enjoyed playing with her. Fucking with her mind, body and emotions. Way more than I ever thought I would. Even more so when I've spent so long fantasizing about her inevitable downfall.

I visualized all the different ways this could play out. Of all the ways I wanted to break her, piece by beautiful piece. Messing with her fragile state of mind until she can't take it anymore. Until she's down on her knees, tears streaming, her body bare and bruised, crying out.... Begging for my mercy. Something which will never come. Pleading with me to stop. To end it all—this wicked game she plays so well, along with her pitiful existence.

"Such a pretty little brat," I whisper. "Such a fucking waste."

I'm not stupid. I know better than anyone that looks can be deceiving. Black fucking magic at its finest. The darkest kind. Built up to hold so much power, the ability to lure in your victim, pulling them closer under false pretenses while perfectly masking the demon hidden from view. Silently simmering just below the surface.

I know this because I'm the master of deceit. Something I perfected long ago, along with many of my other hidden talents. Talents this brat will soon discover.

A soft moan escapes her parted lips as she falls deeper, catching me off guard as she slowly succumbs to the darkness. Struggling to fight the drowsiness as it pulls her under, taking her innocent and vulnerable mind to places she'll never remember. Totally oblivious to the monster standing just inches from her, lurking in the shadows. Oblivious to the wicked and degrading acts I do to myself and her body when it's just the two of us. Getting off on the fact that she has no way of stopping me.

I'm a monster. "What happens in this room stays in this room, isn't that right, princess?" I mutter, my heated breath grazing her lips. Just knowing there's a small chance she can hear me but can't fight me off, it drives me fucking crazy.

Her body is mine to do as I please. Savage property 'til the end. Fuck, most chicks would give up their soul to experience a taste of what this ungrateful brat has. I'll be honest, there have been times where I've come close—too fucking close to derailing the plan. Sending this freight train straight off the track. My mind gets consumed, overshadowed by the thought of her. The very essence of her, causing me to falter. Making me forget all about my endgame.

I've been ready to expose the beast hidden beneath the mask. More than happy to teach this brat a lesson or two while she's conscious. More than happy to show her what monsters are really capable of. And I mean real monsters. Not some Disney make-believe bullshit. I'm talking about the ones who wait it out in silence. Biding their time. Always on the lookout for the perfect moment to strike.

Anti-heroes are child's play. I'm the villain. I'm the real fucking deal and one day soon my sleeping beauty will wake from her spell, and she'll witness me in all of my brutal glory. She'll watch in awe, chained at my side like the obedient bitch she's destined to become, as I take my rightful place on my throne. A throne and kingdom built from the blood and bones of our enemies.

I can't fucking wait for that day to arrive.

The problem I'm faced with right now is dropping the ball. Exposing my plan too soon will limit my playtime with her. I'm constantly telling myself I need to perfect my mission, but the truth is, I'm not ready to deny myself. I've always done things my way and I'm not about to change that anytime soon.

I'm having way too much fun watching her. Playing with her. Exploring her not so innocent body. Then there's the thrill of standing over her as she struggles to breathe—knowing she's suffering because of me. Fuck, it's a feeling I can't even begin to describe. Intoxicating, consuming and powerful as fuck. It gets me so fucking hard every time. Solid as a motherfucking rock.

She's becoming my obsession. A bittersweet addiction. One I know I'll have to give up in the end. I've told myself I can walk away anytime. This stupid bitch doesn't mean anything to me. She's nothing more than a convenient means to an end. When she's finally served her purpose, she'll be no more. Like she never existed. Sent straight back to the earth, dust to dust.

That thought pleases my corrupt mind, but the truth is I'm hooked. Addicted. She's fast becoming my own heavenly brand of crack. My body is constantly craving her touch. Desperate for a hit. Just another fix. Refusing to walk away. Determined to prevent the deadly comedown. The inevitable crash waiting to consume my mind and body. Instead, I keep coming back, foolishly riding the high while I still can—before this fucked up situation comes crashing down around us. Around all of us.

I've gone too far. Overstepped the line in my sick and twisted game. Hellbent on revenge and destruction, but I won't apologize for my actions. Nor the damage caused. This needs to happen, and one day soon it needs to end.

I just don't know how or when.

I pull my dick free and fist my solid length, squeezing hard while palming from root to tip, gliding up and down in slow, deliberate strokes. Leaning in closer, I breathe her in, savoring her sweet vanilla scent while my hand pumps faster, picking up speed as I imagine my free hand wrapping around her throat. Her soft flesh warms my palms as I squeeze with just enough pressure before forcing my dick inside her smart-ass mouth. My hips move automatically as the images consume me. Thrusting deep, filling her completely until she can't take anymore. Until she's gagging. Choking on my dick... almost falling unconscious from her depleting oxygen levels. The feel of her limp and lifeless body going cold on me as I continue to violate every fuckable inch of her.

I could have killed her a handful of times already, and fuck if I haven't come close. As quick as snapping her exposed neck while she sleeps. Cutting a vital artery with a swift nick of my knife or by injecting a lethal dose straight into her veins, making her foam at the mouth; her heart stopping in seconds.

I've thought about it. I've thought about every scenario long and hard. Make no mistake, when I've finished having my wicked way with her, I'll be the one to end it. To end her.

This brat is mine to destroy. I'll take great pleasure in fucking what's left of her while she's still warm. I'll fill her with my cum so she can carry a part of me to the grave—into the next life. A firm and ever-present reminder of her sins, before sending her decomposing body, bloodied and bruised, back to where she came from.

Discarded.

Tossed into a pile. Just another victim in this deadly game of lies, deceit and destruction. Another victim in a long line of many, but this one hits different. This time it's personal. And as much as I want to hurt her, to break her beyond repair, to damage her beyond recognition, I know that disposing of her too soon would be too easy. Too final.

No, playing with her is far more appealing. A welcome challenge and one I couldn't refuse. This is my end game. My rules, played on my terms.

"Caleb," she pants beneath me, my name falling from her lips on a heated whisper. A sound I'm becoming all too familiar with. A sound which speaks to my dark and corrupted soul like no other and I smirk, happy in the knowledge even her subconscious mind can't get enough of me.

I made a promise to myself that while she has air in her lungs and her heart beats freely, she'll never escape my relentless pursuit.

Tracing the outline of her swollen lips, I notice the flush of color rising on her cheeks, emphasizing the small dusting of freckles on her button nose. She looks peaceful as her auburn hair fans across the pillow and I savor it all. Committing it to memory so I can torture myself some more when she's out of my sight—but never my mind.

Some would call her perfect.

Dane and Cameron seem to think so. Admittedly, I can't deny her raw beauty, but I prefer to call it torture. An inconvenience I don't need. A distraction I never saw coming, this brat was sent to me as a challenge. The ultimate test: but what she doesn't know is that I failed that test years ago.

"This isn't your fault, princess." I remind her, as I do every time I creep into her room. "But someone has to pay for what they did. Turns out that someone is you. It has to be you. Sure, it might not seem fair, and even though you'll never truly understand my reasons, you have to trust me. You need to believe this is right and just."

Her body shudders under my touch, her skin temperature dropping as my fingers search her body, traveling south, slowly gliding from her jaw... down her neck before slowing at the base. Pausing to feel the beat of her steady pulse, thrumming gently under my thumb.

Knowing I can end this... snuffing the life out of her at any given moment, fuck it does something wild and feral to me. It feeds my soul—spurring me on. Making my hollow heart come alive, eradicating the emptiness. The detachment I'm forced to carry. If only for a short while.

Continuing south, a sharp hiss escapes me as the curve of her breast fills my palm. So soft. So fucking perfect. I massage it gently before squeezing harder. Her nipple hardens under my touch as I roll and pinch it between my thumb and forefinger, losing myself as a wild and feral need to touch and claim every part of her takes over me, becoming my whole personality.

My dick throbs violently as I continue to caress her soft creamy flesh as it glistens under the moonlight seeping in through the window. A stark contrast against my scarred and callous hands.

Smooth against rough.

Fire against ice.

Every guy's wet dream against her never-ending nightmare.

Who would have thought this feisty brat would be so easy to mold and condition. To become so submissive. Obedient. Such a good fucking girl. Well, she doesn't have much choice right now. Not when she's out cold. But I know my life would be so much sweeter if she was this compliant in the real world. Back in the land of the fucking living. If she behaved while she was conscious then I wouldn't need to drug her as much.

Her breathing slows some more as I continue to chase my release, drawing closer as I fuck my hand, knowing I'll be fucking her dirty little mouth soon enough. Then I'll claim her tight little pussy too and when she calms the fuck down, her ass will be mine too. She'll probably protest, act all offended but the little slut will love every fucking second.

But first this brat needs discipline. She needs to show me how much of a good girl she can be in the big bad world. She needs to prove her loyalty to me and my brothers before she earns that kind of reward.

She moves some more, the sedative not holding its usual effect. I didn't expect her to build up such a tolerance so soon, but I don't allow that to discourage me. I'll just increase her dose tomorrow. An easy fix to a little problem. Her resistance doesn't have to change anything between us—at least not yet.

"Fuck..." I bite out, dragging the small sheet away from her body, tossing it to the floor where it belongs, alongside her innocence. What the fuck is she doing to me?

My balls draw up and I explode, cumming all over her perfect little titties. Showering her. Marking her as mine, even if her conscious mind doesn't know it. Unable to stop myself. Unable to hold back, I bring my hungry lips down to hers and bite hard, piercing her soft flesh.

"Mine," I growl, my tongue darting out and licking away the blood like a possessed animal. Wild and out of control. Like the savage beast I am. The way I was trained and conditioned to be. True to my fucking namesake. "Mine to use. Mine to abuse. Mine to fuck and destroy. To expose and dispose."

And just like that it's done.

I've marked this brat as my own. Dane and Cameron might be having fun with her, but in the end, it will be my hand that destroys her. To them she's just a bit of fun. A hot pussy with a mouthpiece to pass the time, but to me she's more. So much fucking more.

I'm the one with the vicious vendetta. The destructive endgame. A deadly score to settle. Something to prove. That's why I set out to destroy this sleeping beauty long before Dane and Cameron came into my life. Her fate was sealed with my hands and now I'm the monster, silently creeping into her room in the middle of the night. I'm the one who violated her body for my own sick and twisted pleasure. Staking a claim on her. Fueled by an insatiable need. A relentless rage. Hell bent on revenge.

She's the unexpected enemy. A fact we all need to remember, and whether she wants to play a part in my game or not, sooner or later she'll have to face the consequences. This brat will pay the fucking price for messing up my life. For the damage caused. For the sins of others, even if she didn't sign up for it.

Unfortunately for her, mercy doesn't form part of my vocabulary. Foolishly she's the one who walked into my life, putting herself bang in the middle of a brutal war full of lies and destruction. A vicious and constant battle to the death.

A life for a life.

Harsh, maybe... but it's the only way to balance the scales. While she's been dead to the world she made a deal with the devil. Her innocent soul was sacrificed; sealed with her own blood; and she has no recollection of it.

A secret between me and the shadows.

All she'll have is a hazy mind when she finally comes around in the morning. The real monster is still hidden from view, always watching—preying on her every move.

Stepping back, I pull off my mask before retreating into the darkened corner of her room. A mixture of hate and hunger beats ferociously in my chest, my heart fighting against my mind. Giving into her beauty wasn't part of the plan. I have every intention of getting closer, finding the perfect way to get inside her deluded mind, fucking it up—intent on destroying every part of her. But the more time I spend hiding out in her room, the more I'm struggling to walk away unscathed.

I've watched her from a safe distance for years, more than happy to bide my time. Waiting for the perfect moment to strike. But that all changed not too long ago when she turned up here, invading my territory like she has the fucking right. Rubbing her very existence in my face.

I knew then, right in that moment, I had to find a way to claim her. To keep her under my control, I set my newly revised plan into action. Keep her close at all costs. I mean, what's the worst that could happen?

Now she's just millimeters away. Within touching distance and I'm finding it hard, almost impossible to stay the fuck away from her. I'm struggling beyond reason to resist the pull. My mind and body, usually cold and composed, emotionless and empty, are failing to resist the temptation she brings. Something I've never experienced before.

"This won't last forever." I tell myself, not feeling the conviction on my tongue. Hell, this fucked up situation can't last forever. I've worked too hard, sacrificed too much to drop the ball. I've focused most of my life, dedicating it solely to her inevitable downfall....

Yet here she is, laid bare before me. My body responding to her every move, every breath, throwing all my plans out the window like they never fucking mattered.

Get it together, Caleb. I scold myself.

I need to keep my mind focused. I need to keep my head in the game. Constantly reminding myself why I started this to begin with. Reminding myself why this needs to happen. Reminding myself who I am and what I stand for.

I'm Caleb fucking Savage.

King and ruler of Stonebrooke Manor. I'm ruthless, heartless and corrupt to the core. Power fuels my twisted mind. Destruction soothes my darkened soul, and revenge keeps my hollow heart beating, forcing determination through my veins.

One day soon the novelty will wear off. I'm not sure when, but I'll eventually grow tired of sneaking into her room when the lights go out. She'll become all too familiar. Her body predictable and I'll bore easily of the ungodly and unspeakable things I do to her body while she's comatose beneath me.

She'll soon lose her appeal.

In time, this fucked up obsession or whatever it is, will fade away alongside her rotting corpse. The torture, both mental and physical, will be nothing more than a distant yet beautiful memory. Like it never happened.

All that will remain is a deep-rooted rage and a constant thirst for revenge. That will be my moment. My time to shine and when that day comes all bets will be off. I'll have no problem ending her. I'll lure her in, making her fall deeper under a false sense of security before shooting my shot. Striking like the venomous predator I was born to be.

I just hope she finds time to enjoy the ride while she can, because this brat's days are numbered. She's living on borrowed time. Time which is depleting by the second.

Find out what happens next here:

www.books2read.com/stonebrookerebels

About The Author

Stephanie Marie is a coffee loving book whore who resides in a little rainy town in Manchester, UK.

If she's not reading or writing, she's busy watching the football with her two boys; one red—one blue. Someone has to play referee, right?

Let's stay connected

If you'd like to hear about upcoming releases and join my arc team please join:

Stephanie Marie's Book Babes

If you'd like to follow me on my socials, you can do that here:

Friend me:

Instagram

Goodreads

TikTok

Printed in Great Britain
by Amazon